Precious Moments of Christmas

By Debbie Wiersma
Illustrated by Samuel J. Butcher

A Golden Book • New York
Western Publishing Company, Inc., Racine, Wisconsin 53404

"He is the Christ Child and his name is Jesus."

 C Is for the Christ Child

Danny's brother, David, was a shepherd, and Danny liked to go to work with him. The soft, furry lambs made such a nice bed when he was tired.

One night Danny was curled up with the lambs, looking at the stars. Was that a new star in the sky? It was the brightest, most beautiful star Danny had ever seen. It seemed to get bigger and brighter the longer he looked at it.

All of a sudden the light was right in front of the shepherds. They all gathered around to see.

"What is it?" David asked. Then the light just disappeared.

"Angels," Danny whispered. "The sky is full of angels."

"Listen to me, shepherds," an angel said. "Tonight a baby was born in a stable in Bethlehem. He is the Christ Child and his name is Jesus." The angel spread his wings and raised his arms. "You have been chosen to welcome the

Christ Child. Someday he will be king of all the Earth, but for now his birth must be kept secret. Remember, shepherds, he is your new king."

When the angel finished talking, he disappeared behind the bright light and slowly floated back up into the heavens.

"What can we do?" David said to his friends. "We are just poor shepherds. What do we have that is fit for a king?"

"But we were only told to welcome him," another shepherd said. "We don't need to bring him gifts."

"We are just poor shepherds. What do we have that is fit for a king?"

"Bringing him our love will be enough," a shepherd said from behind Danny.

But he's our king, Danny thought. I know our love would be enough, but I *want* to do more. I want to make Baby Jesus feel like a real king.

When the shepherds got to the stable, they saw the same beautiful star in the sky.

"That must be the angels watching over Baby Jesus," Danny said.

The shepherds went inside to see the baby. They talked to Mary and Joseph. Nobody noticed that Danny was missing. When they were getting ready to leave, the little boy walked out from behind a stall.

"I made a gift for you," he said to the Christ Child. He pulled a beautiful crown out of his cloak and placed it on Jesus' tiny head.

"This isn't made of silver or gold," Danny said. "But it's my way of telling you that I really do believe you are my king."

On that cold winter night, Baby Jesus smiled for the very first time. And his smile was for a poor shepherd boy named Danny.

"I made a gift for you," he said to the Christ Child.

 Is for Heart

Angie turned her piggy bank upside down and shook out all the money. She was going Christmas shopping with her best friend, Becky.

"Let's see," she said to Becky. "I've got $29 altogether. Wow! That's a lot of money."

She put the money in her purse, and they went out to catch the bus.

At the shopping mall, Angie saw a huge Christmas tree covered with little hearts.

"What's that?" she asked a boy who was caroling near the tree.

"It's called a giving-tree," the boy said. "Each of these little hearts has a child's name on it. You take a heart off the tree, buy them a little gift, and put it under the tree for Christmas."

"But why?" Becky asked.

"These children's parents can't afford to buy them anything this year," the boy said. "So we are hoping other people will help them to have a good Christmas."

"These children's parents can't afford to buy them anything this year...."

The two friends walked away from the tree to continue their shopping.

"You know," Angie said, "I bet my little brother would love to get my old radio for Christmas."

"And my dad would like a new drawing from me for his office wall," Becky added.

Angie smiled. "I could make my dad's favorite cookies and wrap them up nice. And if I decorated an empty juice can, Mom could use it as a pencil holder."

"Are you thinking what I'm thinking?" Becky asked her friend.

Angie nodded. "Let's go take some hearts off that tree!"

The girls picked five hearts each. One side said "Thank you for sharing your love with me," and the other side had a child's name and age.

Angie and Becky had never had more fun buying anything than they did that day. They knew that they would never see the children who would receive the gifts, but that didn't matter. They would be filling an unknown child's heart with happiness on Christmas, and that child would know that someone's heart was filled with love for them.

"I could make my dad's favorite cookies and wrap them up nice."

 # R Is for Remembering

Jonny pulled one more piece of tape off of the roll and used it to tape the last flap of wrapping paper together.

"I'm all done," he told his mom. "I finished wrapping all my presents!"

"Well, let's see what you have here," Jonny's mom said. "One for Daddy. One for your brother. Here's one for Mommy and one for Grampa. Oh, and this one's for Gramma."

His mom picked up the last gift in the pile. "But, what's this? It says it's to Mrs. Rose. Why did you get her a present, Jonny?"

The little boy smiled. "I like Mrs. Rose, Mommy. She is a nice neighbor. When I go there, she gives me cookies and tea, and she always tells the most wonderful stories. I just want to let her know how much I care about her."

"You make me very proud," Jonny's mom said. She put her arm around her son. "Christmas is the perfect time for remembering

"Christmas is the perfect time for remembering all the people who are special to you."

all the people who are special to you. I'm glad that you remembered Mrs. Rose."

On Christmas Day, Jonny asked if he could go deliver Mrs. Rose's gift.

"In a minute," his mom said. "You helped me to remember something, too."

She went into the kitchen and picked up a huge silver platter. "I remembered that Mrs. Rose won't be able to go out to visit this Christmas, so I made her a nice Christmas dinner. We'll go over to her house together."

When Mrs. Rose opened her door, she was so happy that she started to cry. She opened Jonny's present and had to wipe more tears from her eyes. He had painted a picture of himself and Mrs. Rose having cookies and tea, and he had even made a frame out of cardboard and yarn.

"Oh, it's the most beautiful painting I have ever seen," the old lady said. "I'll hang it in my living room for everyone to see."

Jonny and his mom had to go back home because his grandparents were coming for dinner. But before they went, Jonny's mom laid out Mrs. Rose's Christmas dinner on the table beside her and lit a bright red candle to make it cheery.

"You'll never know how happy you made me today," she said. "Christmas can be a very lonely time if you don't have anyone to share it with." She gave Jonny a hug and a kiss. "I will always remember your kindness. Thank you for remembering a sick lady at Christmas time."

"I will always remember your kindness."

 Is for Innkeeper

"This is the story of the stable in Bethlehem," Mandy read to her doll.

"'Look over there,' Mary said to Joseph. 'I think I see Bethlehem.'

"In the distance Joseph could just make out the twinkling lights of a city. It was a cold night, and Mary was going to have her baby any time now. Joseph tried to make his old donkey walk faster.

"'We'll have a real bed to sleep in soon,' he said to his wife. When they got to Bethlehem, Joseph went to the first inn that he saw. 'We would like a room, please,' he said.

"'All full!' the innkeeper told him, and he slammed the window shut in Joseph's face.

"At the next inn, Joseph knocked on the window. 'Please, sir,' he said. 'My wife is going to have a baby tonight. We need a room!'

"'Not my problem,' said the innkeeper. 'Go away!'

"This is the story of the stable in Bethlehem."

"There was one more inn to try. The innkeeper was right at the window.

" 'My wife is having a baby,' Joseph said. 'Please let us have a room. Just for the night.'

"The innkeeper shook his head sadly. 'I'm sorry,' he said. 'The king told everyone in the land to go back to their homeland. He has census takers counting every person in the land.' He peeked out the window at Mary. 'You won't find a single room in Bethlehem.'

"Mary looked like she was ready to cry. The innkeeper said, 'Wait right there,' closed his window, and went outside.

" 'I have a stable out in the back where I keep my animals,' he said. 'It's not beautiful, but it is very warm. There is straw and blankets and I will bring you food.'

"Joseph smiled and hugged Mary tight. 'That sounds perfect,' he said.

"The innkeeper led them into a stable and helped Joseph make a bed of straw. It felt wonderful to Mary, who had been riding the donkey all day.

" 'Thank you so much for caring,' she told

the innkeeper. 'I don't know what we would have done without you.'

"A little while later Baby Jesus was born inside a warm barn filled with the happy sounds of the animals. And it was all because of one innkeeper who was kind enough to help two tired travelers on a cold winter night. All that night angels watched over the Holy Family."

"All that night angels watched over the Holy Family."

 Is for Sharing

Early one morning Billy and Janie were playing in the playroom when Daddy walked in.

"Have you thought about what you'd like for Christmas this year?" Daddy asked.

The children looked around the room. There was a train set and a box filled with balls. There was a garage with lots of cars and trucks in it. There was a dollhouse and dolls. They saw toys everywhere they looked. One big shelf was full of books and another full of games. Most important, Billy had Teddy. He just couldn't think of anything that he wanted.

"You don't have to get me anything," he said. "I've got everything I need, too," said Janie.

Daddy smiled. "But it makes me feel good to be able to share with you. I like spending my money on nice things for my favorite little boy and girl. How about our taking a ride to the store so you can look around?"

The store was brightly lit with Christmas

Most important, Billy had Teddy. He just couldn't think of anything that he wanted.

lights and decorations. Everyone seemed so happy and excited. Billy and Janie were caught up in the excitement, and they started picking out gifts for themselves.

Then Billy looked out the window and saw a very sad little boy. The boy looked cold, and his clothes were old and torn.

"Daddy," Billy said. "What's wrong with that little boy?"

Daddy said, "He's very poor, and he probably won't have a nice Christmas this year."

Billy felt terrible. He wanted to make that little boy happy. He wanted to make him smile.

"We could share our presents with him," Janie told Daddy. "You mean you'd give *all* your Christmas presents to that little boy?" Daddy asked.

Billy headed toward the door. "That's right, Daddy. We *want* to share."

Daddy watched through the window as they went outside. The poor little boy's face lit up like the Christmas lights around him. He had such a big smile on his face when Janie gave the presents to him.

On the way home, Daddy said, "I saw how happy it made you to share today. It made me decide to share, too. Tomorrow we'll go to the grocery store and buy food and decorations. You can take them to school and ask your teacher to see to it that every needy family has a Merry Christmas."

"It's nice to be able to share, Daddy," Billy said. "It's the happiest feeling of all."

The poor little boy's face lit up ... when Janie gave the presents to him.

 Is for Tree

"Why do we decorate trees for Christmas?" Tammy asked her big brother.

Timmy didn't want to admit that he didn't know the right answer, so he made one up.

"Well, one day a long, long time ago," he began, "there was a little boy named Tobey. Tobey was taking a walk in the woods by his house when he saw his little bird friend. The bird was putting little twigs in a pine tree."

"Was she making a nest?" Tammy asked.

"Yes," said Timmy, "but she was building it in a very small tree. A big gust of wind came and knocked the tree right down. Tobey felt so bad for the bird that he brought the little tree with the nest into his house. He put it in a big pot with some water and showed the bird where it was. 'You'll be nice and warm in here,' Tobey told her. 'But we'll have to make your tree look pretty for Christmas. If we don't, Mom and Dad might make me put it outside.'

"Why do we decorate trees for Christmas?"

"So Tobey took some pretty berries and his mother's yarn and decorated that tree until it looked beautiful. 'I don't want you to get homesick,' he told the bird. 'So I will put a star on top of the tree. That way it will be just like you're outside.' He made a star out of gold paper and put it on top of the tree. When his mother came in and saw it, she said, 'What a beautiful tree. That's the prettiest Christmas decoration I've ever seen.'

"'We should do this every year,' Tobey's father said. And pretty soon everyone had heard about Tobey's Christmas tree."

"Boy," Tammy said. "You know everything. Don't you?"

Timmy just smiled and shrugged. Well, it *could* have happened that way, he thought. Couldn't it?

"A big gust of wind came and knocked the tree right down."

M Is for Merry

"Mommy?" Angie asked. "You know when people say, 'Have a Merry Christmas'?"

Mommy said, "Yes. Why?"

"Well, I don't know what that means," the little girl said.

"Merry Christmas?" asked Mommy. "I guess it means to have a fun day."

Angie sat down at the kitchen table. "So merry means fun?"

"Well, not really," her mom explained. "It's more like happy. Or happy and having lots of fun and making other people happy all at the same time."

"Oh," Angie said. "Mom?"

"What, Honey?"

"Could I be merry today, even though it's not quite Christmas?"

"Of course you can, Angie!" Mommy said, laughing. "Why don't you see if you can be the merriest Angie in town?"

The little girl ran upstairs to get dressed. When she was ready, she skipped out the front door to be merry.

The people who lived next door didn't have any children. Angie skipped up to their front porch and rang the doorbell.

"Hi, Mrs. Smitty!" she said. "I'm being merry today. Do you need any help with anything?"

Mrs. Smitty smiled at the happy little girl. "You could help me bring the garbage out to the curb," she said.

Angie took a big trash bag and pulled as hard as she could. She sang all the way out to the curb. "La, la, la, la, la!" When she was done, she turned and saw Mrs. Smitty watching her.

"I've never seen anyone that happy about taking out the trash," she said. "I guess it can be a fun job. Seeing you this happy makes me want to skip and sing, too!"

Together, Angie and Mrs. Smitty skipped over to Old Phillip's house singing, "La, la, la, la, la!"

"Old Phillip," Angie asked, "can we help you with anything?"

"You can help me with the Christmas decorations," the old man said.

"Why don't you see if you can be the merriest Angie in town?"

Angie and Mrs. Smitty decorated the porch with holly and sang, and pretty soon Old Phillip was singing, too.

"Why's everyone so happy?" asked Angie's friend Paul, just coming up the sidewalk.

"I was being merry, and it made other people want to be merry, too," said Angie with a merry laugh.

In just a few minutes Old Phillip's yard was full of neighbors and friends singing, "La, la, la, la, la!" Everyone had such a happy feeling in their hearts that before they left, Angie said, "Let's have a merry day more often! I never knew how much fun it could be!"

Everyone laughed and said, "What a good idea!"

And as they left Old Phillip's house, each and every one of them shouted, "Merry Today to you!"

Angie and Mrs. Smitty decorated the porch with holly and sang....

 # Is for Angel

This was little Chris's first year in the Christmas play. He was so excited when Mikey handed him his script. But when he looked at it, he couldn't find anything underlined. He wasn't supposed to say a single word!

"I don't want to be an angel," he told Mikey. "I want an important part." Mikey scowled at him. "You *have* to be an angel. Next year you can have a better part."

Little Chris was sad. An angel who didn't talk just didn't seem like a very good part. "I guess I'll just be the best angel I can," the little boy said sadly.

On Christmas Eve all the families in the neighborhood came to see the Christmas play. Mikey was playing Joseph, and his best friend, Lisa, was playing Mary. It was almost time for the angel to come out, and little Chris was getting nervous.

Mikey was playing Joseph, and his best friend, Lisa, was playing Mary.

"There sure are a lot of people out there," he told a shepherd standing next to him. "I hope I do a good job."

And then it was time. Little Chris was Baby Jesus' guardian angel. He stood near the manger and shined his light down at the beautiful baby.

When the play was over, he ran to tell his mom how happy he was. Just as he got there he heard Mikey's mom say, "Oh, Mrs. Bursley, you must be so proud of little Chris. He was a perfect angel."

"Mommy," he said. "I had the most important part in the play. I never knew how important the angels were before."

He had the biggest smile on his face. "I was so proud to be Baby Jesus' guardian angel. I hope I get the same part next year!"

Little Chris put his hand in his mom's and said, "Because what would Christmas really be without the angels?"

"I was so proud to be Baby Jesus' guardian angel. I hope I get the same part next year!"

 **Is for Song**

Sammy and Stevie were walking along a brightly lit street singing Christmas carols they had been practicing for weeks.

"We wish you a merry Christmas, we *wish* you a merry Christmas," they sang loudly. "We *wish* you a merry Christmas, and a happy New Year!"

Sammy turned to Stevie. "I'm a *much* better singer than you," he said.

"Oh, no," Stevie said. "You're wrong. My voice is lots better than yours."

Just then Sarah and Cindy came around the corner. "Away in a manger. No crib for a bed," the little girls were singing. "The little Lord Jesus lay down his sweet head."

"Hi, Sarah," Sammy called out. "Hi, Cindy."

When the girls came over, Stevie said, "Sammy thinks he sings better than I. I sing best, don't I?"

Cindy shook her head. "My mother says I have the most beautiful voice in the world."

Sammy and Steve were...singing Christmas carols they had been practicing for weeks.

"I sing better than all of you," Sarah said.

"No, you don't!" Sammy shouted. "I do!"

Soon all four children were arguing loudly.

"Excuse me!" a voice said. The children stopped arguing and looked up. Mr. Jones was standing in the doorway of his doughnut shop.

"What is going on out here?" he asked them.

"We're trying to decide who has the best voice," Cindy said.

Mr. Jones smiled. "Well, none of your voices sounded very pretty when you were arguing. Why don't you come inside for a doughnut and hot chocolate. I'd like to talk to you."

The four children sat at an empty table with their treats, and Mr. Jones pulled up a chair.

"You see," he said. "Everyone has a different voice. Some can sing way up high and some can sing really low. Some have deep voices and some sound just like little birds. How do think a group of singers would sound if they all had the same voice? It would be pretty boring." He stopped long enough to sip some cocoa. "Songs aren't for seeing who's better, they're for showing everyone how happy you feel inside. As long as you are happy when you sing, then no one is singing better than you."

When the children finished their doughnuts, Stevie said, "I bet it would sound twice as pretty if the girls came with us to sing Christmas carols."

And that night, everywhere along the street, people came out on their porches to see who was singing such beautiful songs.